Library Girl

How NANCY PEARL Became America's Most Celebrated Librarian

Karen Henry Clark Illustrated by Sheryl Murray

little bigfoot
an imprint of sasquatch books
seattle, wa

For Cliff, of course —KHC

For Aunt Jeanne, who has always
made me feel seen —SM

ACKNOWLEDGMENTS

With appreciation to Mark Bowden, Coordinator for Special Collections,
Burton Historical Collection at Detroit Public Library —KHC

Manufactured in China by Printplus Ltd. in May 2022

LITTLE BIGFOOT with colophon is a registered trademark
of Penguin Random House LLC

26 25 24 23 22   9 8 7 6 5 4 3 2 1

Editor: Christy Cox
Production editor: Bridget Sweet
Designer: Anna Goldstein

Photo credits (page 32):
Nancy Pearl with bicycle: © Nancy Pearl
Nancy Pearl with books: © Kevin Clark / The Herald
Nancy Pearl action figure: © Archie McPhee

Library of Congress Cataloging-in-Publication Data

Names: Clark, Karen Henry, author. | Murray, Sheryl, illustrator.
Title: Library girl : how Nancy Pearl became America's most celebrated librarian / Karen Henry Clark ; illustrated by Sheryl Murray.
Description: Seattle, WA : Little Bigfoot, an imprint of Sasquatch Books, [2022] | Audience: Ages 5-9. | Audience: Grades K-1.
Identifiers: LCCN 2022003142 | ISBN 9781632173188 (hardcover)
Subjects: LCSH: Pearl, Nancy--Juvenile literature. | Librarians--United States--Biography--Juvenile literature. | LCGFT: Biographies. | Picture books.
Classification: LCC Z720.P43 C57 2022 | DDC 020.92 [B]--dc23/eng/20220215
LC record available at https://lccn.loc.gov/2022003142

ISBN: 978-1-63217-318-8

Sasquatch Books
1325 Fourth Avenue, Suite 1025
Seattle, WA 98101

SasquatchBooks.com

Nancy loved reading more than recess.

Whenever she tried talking about books, kids ignored her.

Or they shouted, “Go away, library girl!”

This made Nancy sad.

Why do they tease me about the library? she wondered.

The school library held Nancy's best friends—
all those characters tucked into pages.
She never felt lonely reading their stories.

LIBRARY

So, of course, the school library was Nancy's favorite place.

She visited after class to talk about books with Miss Glenn, the librarian.

"I wish I could come here on Saturdays," Nancy sighed.

"The public library is open. There's one near you."

Miss Glenn drew a map.

Hope fluttered like pages turning in Nancy's heart.

On Saturday, Nancy studied the map with her bicycle that she'd named Charger.

She loved pretending he was a beautiful horse.

"This will be a big adventure—just like in a book," she explained.

As Nancy raced down the sidewalk, her imagination soared.

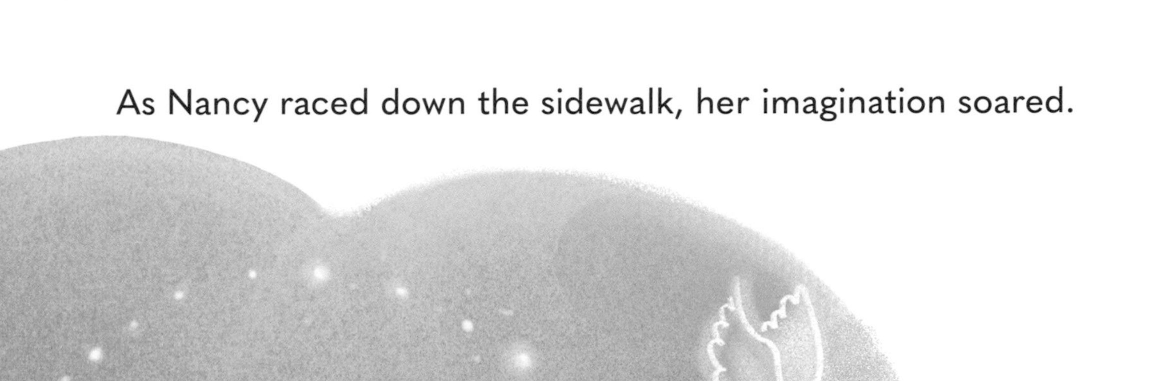

"Onward, my fearless steed!" she cried.

to the FRANCIS PARKMAN BRANCH LIBRARY

When they arrived, Nancy stared at the library for a long time.

"Charger, this whole building is filled with books!"

The stone faces and owls winked.

Nancy thought she was dreaming.

Inside, two librarians greeted Nancy.

"Are kids allowed in here?" she asked.

They smiled.

Nancy felt certain the stone lions did too.

"What do you like to read?" Miss Whitehead asked.

"Horse books!"

"Come with us," said Miss Long.

They showed Nancy a room with enough books to build a bridge to the moon.

She planned to read them all.

The next Saturday, Nancy returned on Charger.

Beneath the stained-glass window, she found a stack of books with a note:

Nancy,

When you finish these, I have a new horse book for you.

Miss Whitehead

Nancy had to hide with these books. Otherwise, kids might pick on her.

Then she saw the table, surrounded by magic light.

I'll be invisible under here, she believed.

By closing time, she'd read the stack and claimed the new horse book.

Every Saturday, Nancy and Charger arrived when the library opened.

She read through rows of
fantasies, trilogies,
diaries, anthologies,
dictionaries, histories,
biographies, and mysteries.

I can be anything when I grow up, she discovered.

One day, Miss Whitehead asked, "Nancy, would you like to give a talk about horse books to other kids?"

"No," she answered. "They'll make fun of me."

"You're an expert," Miss Long said. "You've read all our horse books."

"What helps you feel brave?" Miss Whitehead asked.

Nancy wasn't sure. She was afraid, but she didn't want to disappoint the librarians.

They believed in her.

Finally, she agreed.

Brave was never how she felt around other kids.

What if I'm boring?
What if they laugh?
What if no one comes?

The library had become the place where she belonged.

Failure would destroy that.

The night before the event, Nancy couldn't sleep.

She thought about Miss Whitehead's question.

Charger helped her feel brave, but he couldn't go inside.

But my toy horses can! she realized.

The next morning, with the toy horses in a box, Nancy climbed on Charger.

But managing both was too difficult.

She lost her balance and over they went.

The neighborhood milkman rushed toward her. "Nancy! Are you all right?"

"Yes, but Charger's hurt! I have to speak at the library, and I can't walk fast enough to get there on time. What should I do, Mr. Fishoff?"

"Gather the horses while I put Charger on your porch to rest. I'll drive you."

And they zoomed away.

When Nancy faced the library audience, nerves nibbled at her.

But she had to be calm.

Horses could sense fear.

A stampede was the last thing she needed now.

"Let's make Charger proud," she whispered to her toy herd.

With her hand on a pretty pinto, she began her talk.

All the kids listened, spellbound.

When she finished, they applauded.

Miss Whitehead and Miss Long glowed.

On that glorious day, when the audience was gone,
even the building celebrated Nancy's success.

Nancy's Saturdays changed.

Kids circled around her with questions about books.

She didn't need a magical hiding place anymore.

Nancy had found her own magic.

She knew what she wanted to do when she grew up—become a librarian.

And she did.

Because reading, Nancy knew, helped
people find dreams of their own . . .

with the turn of every page.

AUTHOR'S NOTE

Above, left to right: Nancy and Charger prepare to gallop to the library, Nancy loves books, Nancy is the model for Archie McPhee's librarian action figures

Books magically expand worlds every day. Librarians watch it happen—reader by reader.

That was a great experience for Nancy (Linn) Pearl, born in 1945 in Detroit, Michigan, when she discovered the Francis Parkman Branch Library. There, children's librarian Frances Whitehead recognized Nancy's book brilliance and devised a plan to build her self-confidence.

By the time Nancy turned ten, becoming a librarian was her ambition. She graduated with a master's degree in library science from the University of Michigan. Aside from serving as a public librarian in Detroit, Michigan, and Tulsa, Oklahoma, Nancy worked at Yorktown Alley Bookstore in Tulsa's Utica Square.

Her career exploded when she became the executive director of the Washington Center for the Book at the Seattle Public Library in 1993. This position launched her as a public speaker, author, teacher, consultant, critic, host of TV's *Book Lust,* and contributor to NPR's *Morning Edition.*

She founded "If All of Seattle Read the Same Book" in 1998 to promote community discussions about a chosen book, a program now embraced internationally.

Once challenged to write a six-word memoir, Nancy wrote: "Girl discovers books, then discovers life."

Now retired, Nancy continues her work independently and enjoys long walks in Seattle, rain or shine. She maintains her passion for reading, contending it is her favorite achievement because it allows her to be anyone and to travel anywhere.

Best of all, she promotes the power of librarians to work magic—reader by reader.

AWARDS

Women's National Book Association Award 2004
Library Journal Librarian of the Year 2011
Pacific Northwest Booksellers Association Lifetime Achievement Award 2011
King County Library System Foundation Literary Lion Award 2011
National Book Foundation Literarian Award for Outstanding Service to the American Literary Community 2021

ADULT BOOKS BY NANCY

Book Lust four-book series
George & Lizzie
The Writer's Library: The Authors You Love on the Books That Changed Their Lives, coauthored with Jeff Schwager

SPECIAL RECOGNITION

Starbucks cup #169: Nancy Pearl's Reading Rules
Archie McPhee's three Nancy Pearl librarian action figures
Amazon Book Lust Rediscoveries series
Full Tilt Ice Cream flavor
"Nancy" the digital librarian for the National Library of Norway